The *Mystery* of
Pony Hollow

By Lynn Hall

Illustrated by Ruth Sanderson

A STEPPING STONE BOOK

Random House  New York

Library of Congress Cataloging-in-Publication Data
Hall, Lynn.
    The mystery of Pony Hollow / by Lynn Hall ; illustrated by Ruth Sanderson.
    p.   cm.
    "A Stepping Stone book"
    Summary: While exploring her family's new farm on her pony, Sarah stumbles upon a skeleton and a supernatural mystery involving the ponies who lived there many years ago.
    ISBN 0-679-83052-9 (pbk.)—ISBN 0-679-93052-3 (lib. bdg.)
    [1. Ponies—Fiction.   2. Animal   ghosts—Fiction.   3. Ghosts—Fiction.
4. Mystery and detective stories.] I. Sanderson, Ruth, ill. II. Title.
    PZ7.H1458My   1992
    [Fic]—dc20   91-29861

Contents

1
The Hidden House

Sarah was full of Saturday joy. She was up and out into the morning before her mother's banty rooster announced the day.

She had reasons to be happy. It was Saturday, a day in May. And in the pony stable, Panda waited. Sarah raced across the sunny farmyard, taking high jumps over nothing.

The farm was much like others in this part of south central Iowa. It had a square white house, red hillside barn, and a flock of small sheds and outbuildings. But there were two things that made this farm special.

One was the old mine, in the hillside behind the house. The mine had been closed
for more than forty years, and the entrance
boarded over for safety, but Sarah liked
knowing it was there.

The other different thing about the farm
was the pony stable, Sarah's stable. At least
she loved to pretend it was hers. It was a long,
low green building surrounded by white
fenced paddocks. So little paint was left after
all these years that both the green and the
white were mostly gray. Weeds taller than
Sarah grew around the stable, and pigeons
flew in and out through broken windows.

Inside the stable were dust and junk and
pigeon feathers. Everything was cluttered
except one stall, the biggest of the box stalls.
Early this spring Sarah had cleaned that stall
to a shine, for Panda.

Panda nickered as Sarah opened the stall
door. The pony was black, with high white
boots and a wide blaze down her face. She
stood thirteen hands high, big for a pony,

small for a horse. She was just perfect for Sarah. Panda had been dreamed of, and prayed for, ever since Sarah could remember. For two summers Sarah worked at every job she could find that people would pay her for. Little by little she earned the money for her horse. Then last winter her father had bought the Makenna farm, where there was room for a horse. And last month Panda became a reality, not just a dreamed-of horse.

Today, for the first time since Panda came, there was no school and no rain. Today was the day to explore Pony Hollow.

While she brushed and bridled Panda, Sarah imagined the stable as it had been when the mine ponies lived there. Each beautiful Connemara pony had its own stall, complete with a gleaming brass nameplate on the door. Calico cats could be found asleep on the tack trunk.

The old brass nameplates were there now. They were black with grime except for the one on Panda's door. Sarah had rubbed it

clean. She found the name "Oberon." She had looked up the word in the dictionary. "King of the fairies," the dictionary said.

Out of the stable, out of her dreams of past ponies, Sarah led the little black mare. She scrambled up onto the mare's woolly back. With a sigh of pure pleasure, she picked up the reins and headed Panda toward the hay field, which was black and plowed and ready for planting. Across the fields they trotted, then turned into a grassy road that went among oak and cedar trees, and down a long slope into Pony Hollow.

Pony Hollow was named for the famous Makenna ponies, imported from Ireland to work in the mines. Other mine owners had laughed at Mr. Makenna for spending so much money to import fancy Irish ponies, but the ponies had made Makenna famous. And the rough valley had become known as Pony Hollow. The man who sold Sarah's parents the farm had told Sarah about it.

"There's nothing down there," he'd said.

"Just timber. The land is too rough to farm. It's not good for much, but it is pretty."

Now Pony Hollow was dark and silent. Huge trees had died and fallen and were covered with vines. The floor of the woods was carpeted with ferns and wildflowers, blue and purple and white.

The road Panda followed ended in a clearing full of stumps. This was where wood was cut for fuel and then hauled up the timber road to the farmhouse, before the modern furnace was put in. No one used the road or visited the clearing these days. On the far side of the clearing, Sarah saw just a trace of an old rutted road going on. She and Panda followed it.

They had gone quite a distance when Sarah noticed an unusually pretty, flower-filled valley down to the right. She turned Panda toward it.

Suddenly Panda froze. Her head came up, her ears stiffened, her breath came in hard puffs.

"Take it easy," Sarah murmured. "There's nothing to be afraid of."

Then suddenly her own heart seemed to stop. Just ahead was a tiny stone house. It was so covered with vines that it was almost invisible in the greens of the forest. The one small window was boarded over. The door was shut.

And yet, very clearly, Sarah heard a horse whinny. She heard the wild kick of angry hooves against wood. The sounds came from inside the house.

Sarah slid off Panda's back. She started to tie the mare to a tree branch, but Panda reared and bolted toward home.

Sarah started to run after her, then stopped.

She could see that the pony was headed in the right direction and could probably find her way. And the horse inside the house was whinnying. It seemed to be calling for help.

Through the high grass and wildflowers she ran toward the house. "I'm coming. I'll let you out," she called.

"Whose horse could be in there?" Sarah wondered as she ran. "No one lives anywhere close. And how could it have wandered in? The door is closed."

She grabbed the door latch and pulled. It wouldn't give.

The whinnying came again, but this time the sound seemed to be fading. Frantically Sarah picked up a stone and hammered at the latch. The rusted metal bent and finally broke. The door swung inward, creaking on old hinges. Sarah stepped in and peered into the dark room. The house was empty.

2
Sarah Begins a Search

As soon as the door opened, Sarah knew there was nothing alive inside the house. Whatever had been making the noise simply wasn't there. The air in the house was chilly and dank. No body heat warmed it, no horse smell perfumed it.

On the floor, just inches from her shoe, was a long white bone. Sarah looked around and saw other long white bones and a skeleton rib cage that sheltered a squirrel's nest. It was a horse's skeleton, she realized.

The dust of years lay over the bones. It took a few minutes of staring for Sarah to recognize the moldered remains of a leather halter lying across the skull. The leather was all but gone, but the rings and buckles remained, green with age. Another bit of metal caught Sarah's attention. Carefully, trying not to touch the bones, she picked it up. She rubbed it with her thumb and felt engraved letters. Then she rubbed it against her jeans, knowing somehow, even before the letters came clear, what they would say.

"Oberon."

She stared down at the skeleton. It was obvious now that this was not a horse but a pony, about the size of Panda. Oberon. One of the Makenna ponies, and evidently the most important of them, judging from the size of his stall in the pony stable.

But what was he doing out here in this hidden valley, a good two miles from home? And how did he die? Was he shut in here deliberately, and if so, by whom?

And above all, where had the sounds come from, the frantic whinnying, the kicking?

"Did I imagine it?" she wondered. "But why would I, when I didn't even know there was an old house down here, or a horse's skeleton? And besides," she realized suddenly, "Panda heard it too. And she was terrified. And I've never seen Panda spook at anything—not ever."

She shook her head and began searching the house. It didn't take long. There were just two small rooms with a dirt floor and walls of rough limestone blocks, three small boarded-up windows, and the narrow door. Sunlight came in from a hole in the roof where overhanging branches had pierced the wood-shingled roof. Outside, creeping vines almost entirely covered the walls and moss covered the roof.

Sarah left, determined now to find out what she could about the Makenna ponies, and Oberon, and how he died. Maybe somewhere in the facts was the answer to the sounds of a trapped horse where no horse had lived for almost fifty years.

At the clearing Sarah found Panda, calm again, grazing. They started for home. Sarah's face wore a frown. The brass nameplate was in her jeans pocket.

Her parents were eating breakfast when she came into the kitchen.

"Wash the horse smell off, and come sit down," her mother said. "Did you have a good ride?"

"Yep." She started to tell them about the house and the skeleton but suddenly decided she didn't want to share it. Not yet.

To her father she said, "Dad, tell me again about the Makenna ponies."

"I already have, at least twenty times."

"I know, but tell me again. Everything you can remember."

He looked at her curiously, but shrugged and said, "They were Connemara ponies, imported from Ireland back in the twenties. Old Makenna—"

"The one who owned the mine," she interrupted.

"The one who owned this place, the mine, everything. He was going to breed pit ponies for the mines. Back then the mining companies around here were too small to use rail systems. Instead, they used ponies to haul the ore cars."

"So he imported Connemara ponies from Ireland," Sarah prompted. "Why did he do that? Weren't there any ponies around here that they could have used?"

"Sure, but old Makenna was the sort of man who had to have everything a little better than anyone else, whether it made sense or not. He spent a fortune on those ponies, even brought over an Irish groom to take care of them. Who ever heard of such foolishness? Pass the bread, Sary."

"Yes, but what happened to the ponies? I know the mines went broke and Mr. Makenna went broke and moved away, but what happened to the ponies? And what happened to the Irish groom?"

Sarah's father shrugged and spread butter

on his bread. "How should I know?"

"I think the Irishman stayed around here somewhere," said Sarah's mother. "Seems to me I heard he went crazy when they sold the ponies, or some such tale. It's been so long, though. Who knows?"

The groom would know what happened to Oberon, thought Sarah. But the ponies were sold almost fifty years ago! He was probably dead by now.

Not necessarily, she argued with herself. If he was a young man when he came over, he would be seventy or eighty years old now.

He might still be around here somewhere, she thought with mounting excitement.

"What was the name of the Irish groom?" Sarah couldn't keep her voice calm. Both parents looked at her oddly.

"Who knows?" Her father shrugged again and said, "Why do you keep asking about it?"

"I just want to know everything about the Makenna ponies."

Her parents knew her well enough to accept this as a logical answer, and the matter was dropped.

That afternoon, after her Saturday housework chores were out of the way, Sarah went up to the attic. She searched all the dusty corners and piles and cartons, hoping to find something left from the time the Makennas lived here, some records, letters, anything that might include the name of the Irish groom. There was nothing.

She wandered down to the stable. Halfway down the aisle, on one side, was a large feed and tack room. Across the aisle was another room that held an iron bed, a broken chest of drawers, a cockeyed table. These must have been the groom's living quarters. Sarah had used this room as her special playing place since her family had moved here. There were no cracks or corners she hadn't already poked into. But she searched it all again, looking for a name.

Nothing. She went back out into the aisle and sat on the tack trunk lid. She felt heavy with disappointment. She could think of no-where else to look.

Suddenly it occurred to her that the tack trunk itself might have come from Ireland with the ponies and the man. This time she braced herself against disappointment as she slid off and opened the lid.

The trunk was empty. She knew it was. But written on the inside of the lid, in ink that was faded almost beyond reading, were words that made Sarah whoop with excitement.

"Property of Aaron Donel, Beckwith Farms, Waterford, Ireland."

3
Some Surprising News

Sarah hung over the bottom half of the stable door and stared into the sunny afternoon. What were the chances, she wondered, of finding Aaron Donel still alive, still in the area? And if she found him, would he know how Oberon had died? Could he explain the sounds?

Sarah closed her eyes and faced, inwardly, the one explanation of those sounds, an explanation she could not believe, for she was the most practical of girls and always had been. Fairy tales bored her, and ghost stories made her snort with contempt. There was

always a logical explanation for a mystery, she told herself.

Except for this one. There was no reason for it. "No one knew I was coming to that place at that time," she thought. "I didn't know it myself. No—"

She shook her head and tried to dodge the only logical explanation. When her parents drove away toward town for their grocery shopping, Sarah went into the house and sat down at the old pine desk in the kitchen. Four small telephone books hardly larger than comic books were stuck in one of the desk's pigeonholes. There was one book for each of the small towns in the area. Sarah pulled them out and began her search.

The first book held no Donels. The second, an Irwin Donel. Sarah marked the page and went on to the third book, fourth book. Nothing. She turned back to Irwin Donel, took a big breath to help hold down her telephone nervousness, and dialed the number.

A woman answered. Feeling a little foolish, Sarah explained that she was trying to locate a Mr. Aaron Donel. Would he be any relation, by any chance?

"Mr. Aaron Donel? No," the woman said, "can't think of an Aaron offhand. It wouldn't be Arthur Donel, over by Drakesville?"

"No, Aaron. He's probably dead by now. Thanks anyway."

So that's the end of that, she told herself.

And she kept thinking of Oberon. How did he die? Why was he in the house? What could the noises have meant?

If Aaron Donel was dead, then who else might know? The Makennas were gone. Or were they?

Back to the phone books she raced. She did not find any Makennas. At supper that night Sarah asked, "Do any of the Makennas still live around here?" No one knew, or was interested enough to give it much thought.

All day Sunday Sarah thought, "I know I've seen that name, Makenna, somewhere. Where was it? A sign? Probably something that had to do with the farm or the mine, that's all. Probably nothing that would help."

It wasn't until Monday afternoon that it hit her. She was walking through the halls at school, on her way back from the lunch-room. Just as she passed the nurse's office it came to her.

Downtown there was a door, between the movie theater and the dentist's office. It led to a stairway, to offices upstairs. On the door in black and gold letters were the words, "Jeanne Makenna, County Health Nurse." Sarah had walked past the door many times, had seen the name, but had had no reason to think of it or to remember it. Till now.

After school she called her mother to say she wouldn't be coming home on the bus. It wasn't a long walk, and Sarah often stayed in town after school and walked home later. She ran the three blocks from school to the remembered doorway.

Through the lettered door and up the stairs she went, slowing down and becoming more timid with every step. A county health nurse was probably a busy person. And probably she wasn't even a relative of the coal-mine Makennas at all.

Sarah was more relieved than disappointed to find the office door closed and locked.

She was turning to go when a woman in a uniform came in the downstairs door.

"Are you looking for me?" the woman asked, puffing a bit as she climbed the stairs. She had a broad friendly face and neat gray hair. Sarah liked her.

"Are you Mrs. Makenna?"

"Miss Makenna," the woman corrected her pleasantly. "What can I do for you?"

Sarah could think of no way to explain why she was there. It all seemed so silly.

Miss Makenna was beside her now, unlocking the door. "Come in." They went into the little green office, and Sarah sat in the chair Miss Makenna indicated.

"Now," Miss Makenna said. "Who are you?"

"Sarah Elgin. I live out at the old Makenna farm."

Miss Makenna looked less businesslike. "Is this a social call?"

"I guess so. I was wondering if you could be any relation to those Makennas, by any chance? I'm trying to find out about the mine ponies they used to have out there, and I couldn't find any Makennas in the phone book."

"I don't live here in town," Miss Makenna said. "Yes, indeedy, I'm related. I grew up out there, as a matter of fact. It was my dad who ran the mine."

Sarah's face relaxed into a happy smile. "Oh," Sarah said softly. "I was so afraid I'd never find anybody who could tell me—do you remember the ponies? Oberon?"

"The mine ponies?" Miss Makenna leaned back in her chair. Sarah held her breath.

"I seem to remember that Dad imported some ponies from someplace. England, I think."

"Ireland," Sarah corrected.

Miss Makenna took a look at her and went on. "Ireland, you're right. Brought a man over from there, too, to take care of them."

"Aaron Donel," Sarah said quickly.

"Yes." Miss Makenna looked at her for an instant. Then she went on. "Dad built a stable for them. It's still standing there, isn't it?"

"Yes." Sarah's eyes shone. "It's a beautiful stable. When I get older, I'm going to fix it all up and be a pony breeder."

"You are, are you?" There was a smile in Miss Makenna's voice, as though she understood about dreams. "Is that why you want to find out about Dad's ponies?"

"Well, it's more than that." Sarah decided quickly that she'd better tell the whole story. "I found the skeleton of one of the ponies. Oberon his name was. And the skeleton was in an old empty house way up in the woods in Pony Hollow, and I'm trying to find out what he was doing up there. How he died." She wished she could tell about the noises,

too, but didn't. That was too much to trust
a stranger with.

"Oberon," Miss Makenna said thoughtfully. "I think that was the stallion. Yes, I
remember him. Beautiful animal, dapple gray
with a mane two feet long." She smiled.

"Can you remember how he died?" asked
Sarah.

"No, I'm afraid not. They arrested Donel
about that time, but I can't recall why. It
had something to do with the ponies, I believe. But I was away at college. I didn't hear
too much about it."

Another dead end, Sarah thought. Her
disappointment was huge. She sighed and
said, "I sure wish I could have talked to Mr.
Donel."

Miss Makenna looked at her for a long
moment. Then she said, "You can, Sarah, if
you want to."

4
A Disappointment

"You mean he's still alive?" It seemed too good to be true.

"He is alive, yes," Miss Makenna answered thoughtfully. "I'm not sure he can answer your questions, though. He hasn't been quite right, mentally, for years. But if you like, I'll take you to see him."

"Yes! Please." Excitement shone all over Sarah's face.

Miss Makenna pondered. "I won't be able to go until this evening. I have some paper work I've got to take care of this afternoon, but if you want to wait around, you can. We'll

pick up a hamburger and go on out to the
nursing home after supper. That's where he
is. Call your parents and tell them where
you'll be."

Sarah spent the rest of the afternoon curled
up on an uncomfortable metal and plastic
couch in Miss Makenna's outer office. She
tried to do her homework, but it was almost
impossible to keep her mind on it. In just a
few hours she'd be talking to Aaron Donel.
The excitement of that thought got in the
way of math and history.

At last Miss Makenna put away her work.
"Come along, we'll get a bite," she said,
as she locked the office. Sarah went down
the stairs with her. They got into Miss
Makenna's car.

By the time they were seated in a booth at
the Burger Barn, Sarah's thoughts were off
in another direction. There was so much she
wanted to ask.

"When you were a little girl, did you ever
go down in the hollow?"

"Oh, yes. My brothers and I spent a lot of time back in there. We hunted mushrooms in the spring and ginseng in the fall. The rest of the time we were just hiding out from doing chores at home."

Sarah grinned, then asked, "Did you know about that old stone house back in there? Did you play in it?"

"Huh," Miss Makenna snorted. "We knew about it all right. My brothers played in it. I didn't. It was the boys' clubhouse. No girls were allowed. They even fixed the door so it locked from the inside, with a wooden bar that dropped down, so I couldn't get in."

"That house was where I found Oberon's skeleton. Maybe Mr. Donel can tell us why Oberon was in the house," Sarah added, before she took a bite of cheeseburger.

Miss Makenna smiled sadly. "Don't count on it. He's been out of touch with reality for a long time now. I stop in to see him from time to time, when I have business to take care of at the home. Sometimes he recognizes me, sometimes not."

Miss Makenna ate slowly and thoroughly, down to her last French fry. Sarah tried to hide her impatience.

It was a long drive, but finally they were there. The county nursing home was a long, low modern building more like a motel than a nursing home. Several old men and women sat in lawn chairs on the grassy slope in front of the building. They seemed to be enjoying the spring evening.

"There he is," Miss Makenna said, pointing, as they got out of the car.

He sat alone, a small silent figure, almost lost in his big, loose overalls. His gray head drooped to his chest. He seemed not to see them coming toward him.

"Evening, Aaron," Miss Makenna called. "I brought you some company."

His head turned slightly toward them. That was all. There was no sign of recognition.

"This is Sarah Elgin, Aaron. She wants to talk to you for a while. I have some things to do indoors," she said to Sarah. "You stay here and talk to him. I'll be right back."

"I've been wondering," Sarah started out weakly. The man seemed not to know she was there. "I was wondering if you could tell me about the Makenna ponies. The ponies you used to take care of?"

He looked away, and behind his eyes he seemed to go blank.

"Could you please tell me about Oberon?" Sarah asked.

There was no response.

"Could you tell me how Oberon died?"

The man was like a doll Sarah had seen once at a craft show. It was a little old man doll with a head that was shaped from a dried apple pinched and worked into a man's features. Aaron Donel stared ahead, lifeless as the dried-apple doll.

When Miss Makenna came back, she and Sarah looked at each other, and the woman shook her head.

"It's no use. Not tonight anyway. Sometimes he's all right, but tonight he doesn't even know that we're here. Come on, I'll take you home."

All the way home Sarah stared out the car window at the farms going by. But she didn't see them. Her mind was fighting Aaron Donel's mind, where the answers were locked up.

"There must be some way to get him to talk to me," she said silently, over and over. "There must be some way."

5
A Dangerous Decision

It was early Saturday morning, and Panda was cross-tied in the stable aisle. She stood patiently dozing while Sarah worked on her with the curry comb. The pony's long winter coat was shedding. The curry comb pulled the hair loose and sent it blowing through the air. Sarah sneezed.

"Where shall we ride today?" Sarah said as she brushed Panda's coat. "We have the whole day. We can go anywhere we want."

But the luxury of a horse of her own and a beautiful spring Saturday were dimmed for Sarah. There was Oberon, out in the stone house. And there was Aaron Donel in the nursing home, with all the answers to the mystery.

"How can I get him to tell me what he knows?" she asked herself for the hundredth time.

Panda stamped and snorted an impatient little snort, as though she had had enough brushing and wanted to get out into the sunlight. Sarah put away the brushes and reached for the bridle.

"You'd help if you could, wouldn't you, Pandy?"

Suddenly she stopped and looked a long thoughtful look at the pony. A pony. A real live, warm pony for Aaron Donel to see and touch and smell. Maybe, just maybe, it would be enough to hold his mind in focus. Maybe Panda could reach him, could touch his memory, as Sarah had failed to do.

"We'll try it," she said. "It might be a crazy idea, and it probably won't work, but we're going to try it."

It wasn't until she was well on her way to the nursing home that she began to have doubts. The excitement of the decision faded as she thought, "How do I go? Maybe I'll get lost and won't be able to find it. No, that's silly. I could ask someone."

But then another problem appeared. When they approached the first farm they had to pass, a large yellow dog came rushing out. He barked furiously. Panda stopped, her ears stiff, eyes wide. Sarah urged her forward and somehow they got past the dog. But Sarah felt suddenly insecure on Panda's back. She had no saddle, and not a lot of riding experience.

At the next farm two dogs came out to bark, but they were smaller, and they didn't come as close. Panda went by them with a nervous dancing step. The next farm had no dog in sight. Sarah began to relax.

But when they turned at the highway and began to ride in the broad roadside ditch, a new worry presented itself. Cars and trucks whizzed by. Panda moved nervously as each one approached, and Sarah tensed. Just then, a huge semitrailer truck roared past, blast-

ing its horn as it went by. Panda leaped, and Sarah landed facedown in the grass.

"Oh no," she groaned. If Panda had run off . . . but the pony had stopped just a few yards away and was grazing. Sarah caught her and jumped back on. A minute later she saw a sign pointing up a road that joined the highway. "Appanoose County Home, 2 miles," it said.

With a loud sigh of relief, Sarah guided Panda across the highway and up the road. Now she had time to worry about what to do when she got to the nursing home.

"What if he isn't outside? I can't ride Panda into the building to look for him. They might not even allow horses on the grounds. Or they might not let me see him. Maybe they have visiting hours."

The last two miles seemed to take hours. But eventually the nursing home appeared. Sarah strained to see if anyone was sitting outside—a small old man in overalls. But the front lawn was empty.

She rode up the gravel drive and halted, not knowing what to do next. A smaller drive led around the building to the back. She reined Panda around and followed the drive. Behind the building were grassy lawns and flower beds. Several elderly men and women moved among the flowers, examining rose bushes, setting out plants, or just enjoying the spring sunshine.

One sunburned old woman walked toward Sarah. "Well, this is quite a surprise," she said, stroking Panda's nose. "What a pretty pony! Where did you come from?"

"We came to see Mr. Donel. Do you know where he is?"

"Mr. Donel? He was here a little bit ago. I'll go see if I can find him for you."

She wandered away. There was a wooden bench beneath a lilac bush. Sarah slid off Panda and sat on it, glad for once to be on solid ground. Her leg muscles ached from the long miles of riding, and her shoulder was stiff from the fall.

At first it was a pleasure to sit in the fragrant shade of the lilac, in spite of her worry about what to say to Mr. Donel. But as the time stretched out she began to worry again. Maybe the old woman had forgotten. Old people get forgetful, Sarah knew. Or perhaps Mr. Donel was having one of his bad days and wouldn't come out. Or maybe—

Suddenly he was there, staring at Panda, moving toward her, reaching out almost hungrily to touch her black coat.

6
Sarah Learns the Secret

"Mr. Doncl?"

He looked at Sarah, and she knew that today the mind behind the eyes was awake.

"Can I talk to you about something?" she asked.

"Depends on what it is." His voice was high and soft and creaky.

"The Makenna ponies."

She couldn't read the emotions that crossed the man's face and then faded. But at least the face wasn't blank.

"This your pony?" he asked, running his hands over Panda's face.

"Yes, sir. I'm Sarah Elgin. I was here the

other evening to see you. I live at the old Makenna place, and I want to find out about your ponies, the ones from Ireland. Would you please tell me about them?"

He looked at her suspiciously. "What are you doing, writing some paper for school?"

She met his eyes. "No, I'm not writing a school paper. I just love ponies. When I grow up, I want to fix up the old stable and breed them—Connemaras, like the Makenna ponies."

As she said it, she knew the dream had been forming in the back of her mind ever since she'd walked into the pony stable and seen the brass nameplates on the stalls.

"You probably know more about ponies than anybody around here," she said simply. "Please tell me about the Makenna Connemaras."

His face lost its suspicion. "Ah, they were lovely," sang the high soft voice. "They were Beckwith bred for generations back. The Good Lord didn't put finer ponies anywhere on this earth, not even in Ireland itself."

He paused and seemed to slip away into a memory.

"What color were they?" Sarah asked gently. She did not want to lose him.

"Dapple grays, most of them. A few bays and chestnuts, but even them had the dappling, like fairy smoke rings, over their quarters. Fine-legged animals they were, and fine small heads with their big dark eyes that could melt your heart into a puddle of Irish rain."

For a moment Sarah almost forgot what she was after. Then, "What color was Oberon?" she asked.

A trembling, like a small electric shock, went through the dried-up little body beside her. Then his voice grew vague. "There was Shannon, she was the best of the mares. Died of a twisted gut, foaling. And Mari, she was lovely. Misty and Morag and Sliante and the two bays, what were their names? Apple, that was one of them."

"And Oberon, was he the stallion?" Sarah pressed on.

"Apple used to get into my bunk room if I didn't latch the door. I had a tin of tobacco in there always, don't you know, on the bureau, and that little mare would steal it every chance she got. Then she'd roll her eyes till I didn't have the heart to take after her for it."

Sarah backed off, then tried another approach. "You must have hated it when the ponies were sold."

"Ah, a black day. You haven't lived long enough to guess at the sorrow. They took my girls away from me. They took my Apple and Mari and the dear others." His eyes looked down, but Sarah could see the tears rolling down the dry old cheeks. Tears welled up in her own eyes.

"Did they take Oberon away too?" she whispered.

The old man sat up and said in a high hard voice, "They would have sent me to the state

prison. I couldn't have lived in prison. Eight days in the county jail was near enough to break me. Years in prison would surely have killed me."

As Sarah waited, her heart pounding, he gripped her arm and stared hard into her eyes. "They were there waiting for me in the stable when I got back. That filthy stableboy told them. He told them he saw me taking Oberon off into the woods, but it was his word against mine. I said Oberon got loose, that I was hunting him, but they didn't believe me. It was the police. It was policemen come to take me away. Grand theft, they called it. Oberon was worth thousands of dollars."

His tired voice caught. Sarah held her breath. "Oberon," the soft, soft voice was back now. "He was the king, all right. The color of an Irish mist, all silver and smoke and devilment. It was me that pulled him out of his dam when he was born, back in Waterford. It was me that put the first baby halter around his wee head and taught him to come along like a gentleman. I taught him all a pony should know, and I taught him more. He could shake hands and count, and he could open almost any door." The voice broke again, and the old man turned away.

"Then of course you couldn't let Mr. Makenna sell him," she said firmly. "I wouldn't have, either."

When he turned back to her, Aaron Donel's face was light and soft and glowing. He held her hand in both of his, but neither of them noticed.

"I should have stayed with him, you see. In the stone house down in the hollow. I should never have gone back to the stable. But I wanted everybody to think Oberon was lost and I'd been out looking for him. I'd told them all I was going to a new job in California. They were expecting me to leave for California the next day.

"My plan was I'd pretend I was on my way to California, and then I'd slip back down into the hollow and get Oberon and sneak away with him. Then Oberon and I would be free, and we'd be together.

"But I did go back to the stable that night, and they were waiting for me, police and all. Then when I was in jail, I was afraid to tell anyone where Oberon was. They'd have known I stole him, and I'd have gone to prison for the rest of my life. I couldn't stand that."

"So you let him die." Sarah didn't know the words were coming out until it was too late. She felt sorry the moment she said them.

The old man cringed away from her and wailed, "No, he won't die. He won't die. He can get out of any door. I taught him. I'll go back as soon as no one is watching, and Oberon will be waiting for me in the valley. There's food and water, and plenty of it. He won't die."

Sarah stood up. She turned to gather Panda's reins, but the man's hands were clutching at her.

"Let him out for me. Please. Let him out."

The pain and guilt of fifty years were written in the lines on Aaron Donel's face. Gently she said, "I already have."

7

A Quiet Farewell

School took over Sarah's life for the next week, so that a ride to Pony Hollow was out of the question. But she used her evenings to get ready for her next visit. With the help of her father, she made a redwood grave marker. She labored long and carefully over the special letters. Oberon's memorial mustn't look like a child's poster.

The marker said, "Here lies Oberon, King of the Connemaras. Born, Waterford, Ireland. Died, Centerville, Iowa. Oberon was loved by Aaron Donel."

Her parents knew, now, about the skeleton and the little stone house, but not about the sounds she had heard. They were mildly interested at first but soon forgot about it. The orchard was filled with the graves of family pets. If Sarah wanted to ride off into the woods to bury the bones of a horse dead fifty years, it was not really out of character for her. Silly, maybe, but nothing worth objecting to.

On Saturday Sarah loaded the redwood marker and the garden spade over Panda's back and rode away, around the hay field and onto the road that led down and down deeper into the tunnel of trees. She got lost three or four times, beyond the end of the road, before she found the right valley. The vine-blanketed house stood in a shaft of sunlight. The door was open.

In the sunny center of the valley Sarah dug the hole and, making several trips, carried the bones to it. Then she covered them over and propped up the marker with a row of rocks.

She stood up and listened to the silence of the valley. A little distance away, Panda lifted

her head from the tender grass and stared with widening eyes at something near Sarah.

Sarah felt it, too, the presence beside her. The rustling grass might have been imagination. The soft puff of air against her neck might have been the breeze.

But Sarah knew that Oberon was there, and it didn't really matter whether or not such things were possible.

She felt he was trying to tell her something, as Panda did when her empty water bucket got filled, or when she wanted to go just a little faster than Sarah was allowing.

Sarah's smile was gentle. "You're welcome, Oberon," she whispered.

About the Author

"I was horse-hungry and dog-hungry all through my childhood," says LYNN HALL, "and found what I needed in books." The award-winning author of more than 85 books for young readers, she loves writing horse and dog stories above all others. Lynn Hall lives in Elkader, Iowa, where she breeds and shows champion Bedlington terriers.

About the Illustrator

RUTH SANDERSON is the illustrator of more than 50 books, and has recently started writing books for children too. She has always loved horses, so she took special pleasure in illustrating *The Mystery of Pony Hollow.* Ruth Sanderson lives in Ware, Massachusetts, with her husband, two daughters, a cat, a dog, and a horse named Shadow.